CONTENTS

Patience's Box

They came in a cardboard box, like a pair of shoes. *CARE - LIVESTOCK* it said on the outside. It stood on the living-room floor, while out in the garden, Dad fixed up the keep-cage.

Patience sat on the floor beside it, aching to open the lid.

"Now don't go opening that yet," her father had said. "Let's get their place ready first." It was like that story about Pandora, where the woman was forbidden to open the box, because if she did . . . But that box had been full of evil, horrid things, whereas this one . . .

No sound came from inside. What were they doing in there? Were they as

anxious to see their new home as she was to see them? Perhaps they were asleep. Or dead? Dead!

What if they had died on the journey home, shut up in that little box? What if they had run out of air, despite the holes in the lid, and suffocated before they even reached home?

With quick, frightened fingers, Patience pulled the cardboard tabs out of their slots, and opened the lid.

Two white explosions went off in her face, as the contents of the box burst out and upwards. Something stiff banged her face. The shade of the light-fitting went *ping*. The room was full of noisy rustling, and two large yellow dollops appeared on the shiny coffee table.

Patience put her arms over her head, whimpering.

When the noise stopped, she looked
around. The birds were sitting on the
curtain rail, pressed shoulder to shoulder,
bobbing their heads in agitation, and
peering at her with eyes the same colour
as the plops on the table. She glanced out
of the window.

Her father was up the stepladder, balanced precariously, with a mouthful of nails, and a hammer in the crook of his arm. There was nothing for it: she would have to try and get the doves back into the box, or she would be in big trouble.

So she climbed on a chair and reached
out for one of the doves. They both took
off with a noise like flapping washing, and
nearly knocked her off the chair. Then
they settled on the carpet, and strutted
about, chests puffed out, like two
indignant little duchesses. More yellow
slime oozed onto the carpet. Patience bit
her lip.

She took off her cardigan and, creeping as close as she dared, threw it over one of the birds. The other took off, pinging the lampshade again and knocking an ornament off the TV. But Patience had tight hold of the other.

It felt horrible: little sharp claws, folded wing-bones as tiny as spillikins, its whole insides palpitating through its frail, white skin.

But she got it back into the box – just as her mother came into the room.

"You opened the box," said her mother coldly, taking in with one glance the bird on the standard lamp, the mess on the furniture. "I do hope you are going to have the patience to own these pets. I do hope we have not misjudged you, Patience," she said, in her dark, alas-for-all-bad-children voice. "I do hope you are going to have enough patience for owning a pet."

"Yes, Mum," said Patience. "Can you help me get the other one down? Please?"

The dovecote had stood in the centre of the garden ever since they had moved in: a beautiful white spire, with little Norman windows cut into the wooden belfry at the top. The idea of white doves fluttering to and fro in the air around it had thrilled Patience from the very first. Over and over she had asked to be allowed to buy doves – "I'll use my own money!" – to live in the white dovecote. Now, at last, that they had found a breeder, and fetched back a pair of fantail doves, along with a keep-cage and feeding troughs, booklets about pigeon diseases and sheets of instructions about bird care, it was not quite as she had imagined.

For one thing, Dad had to attach a great big, ugly keep-cage to the side of the dovecote to keep the doves inside until they came to think of Beam End Cottage as their home. Otherwise they would just fly straight back to the breeder (or try, and get lost on the way).

"Won't they be sad, all cooped up in there for weeks on end?" she said, as Dad folded away the stepladder.

"So long as they get their food and water, they'll be fine," said Dad. "Which means, Patience, that they are depending on you from now on!"

Free at Last

2

So every morning, and as soon as she came home from school, Patience mixed the seed, got out the ladder, and climbed up to the keep-cage and opened the little mesh door, so as to fill the feeding trough and replace the drinking water for her doves.

"Hallo, Noah," she said. "Don't you upset yourself, Nelly. I've just brought you your lunch. No need to get yourself in a state." And the doves would boggle at her and push their little heads in and out, and putter like angry old ladies in a queue at the supermarket.

Shouldn't be allowed, they seemed to say. *Disgusting! Outrageous! Well, did you ever!*

At school, Mrs Clarke invited Patience to tell the class about her new pets.

"Fantails . . ." she said ". . . white all over with tails like a hand of playing cards. The male is bigger then the female. And they kiss all the time . . ."

"Blch," said Eric Bindy.

"Can they carry messages tied to their legs?" asked Maurice Tyler. "Go behind enemy lines?"

"No," said Patience.

"Are you going to race them?" asked Paula Briggs.

"No. They aren't racing pigeons," said Patience.

"Well, what do they *do* exactly?" asked Philip Harris.

But Neesha understood. She was Patience's best friend. "They are beautiful," she said, when she came round to play after school. "They're like sugar mice with wings. They're the souls of little animals flying up to heaven. They are nearly as beautiful as my cat, Tiger. No wonder Noah chose a dove."

That was why Patience had decided on Noah and Nelly for names, though she had always thought to call the doves pretty names like Melody and Marguerite.

The keep-cage was made of wire mesh –
an oblong pen, like scaffolding spoiling
the shape of a lovely church spire. And
when the doves came out onto the deck of
the cage, the mesh looked so hard on their
claws that Patience wanted to rip it away,
and set Noah and Nelly free – free to walk
on the soft grass, drink from the bird-bath,
hop in among the hydrangea bushes.

By the end of five weeks, their beautiful fans of tail feathers had become dirty and stained, and the dovecote smelled. Noah and Nelly came outside to do their business, but it all got stuck to the wire mesh, so that Patience had to clean it off with a wire brush. Their lovely fantails no longer looked like suger mice with wings, but like bedraggled toilet brushes.

And yet Patience knew that if she took off the cage too soon, Noah and Nelly might fly out of her life for ever.

At the end of six weeks, her mother said, "Well? Is it time?"

But Patience said, "I'll wait another week."

At the end of seven weeks, her father said, "Right. Shall I take the keep-cage down today?"

But Patience said, "Another week won't hurt."

Up and down the ladder she went, and never missed once – even though, when it was raining, the rain ran off the dovecote roof in a sharp, cold trickle, straight down her neck as she balanced on the top of the ladder, filling the feeding troughs.

At last, after eight weeks, Patience laid her spoon down beside a half-eaten bowl of cereal. "Tonight, Dad, if you don't mind. Could you take the keep-cage off tonight?"

At school she had trouble concentrating. The numbers in the long-division boxes looked like birds in a cage; the numbers on the top looked like free ones. She ran all the way home. For the last time, the stepladder came out, and this time Patience's father went up, pliers and hammer in hand.

"Don't fret, Noah; he isn't going to hurt you," called Patience. "Calm down, Nelly. He's just going to let you out."

While Dad banged and wrenched and teetered on the ladder, the birds huddled out of sight in the dark recesses of the dovecote. For long minutes after he came down, they stayed hidden from sight. Then their heads poked out at the tiny door – they could turn their heads so far round that it seemed they must come unscrewed. Then their breasts came out, and little claws, to grip the sill. The doves moved so much as one that they looked like one bird standing alongside its own reflection in a mirror.

Suddenly Noah dropped down – a clumsy, fussy jump, like a parachutist whose chute has not opened properly. He squatted in the middle of the lawn for a moment, then cocked his head to one side, as if to summon Nelly. Nelly flumped down beside him. They pecked half-heartedly at the grass. Patience knew they were watching her, her father and mother for some ambush, some act of treachery.

Patience took one step forward . . . and both doves clambered into the air.

Like little yachts, sails fatly swollen, they moved across the blue of the sky. Then, after making one circle of the house, they set off across the fields, across the river, towards the wood.

"Noah! Come back! Nelly!" called Patience.

"They'll be back in a moment," said her mother in a voice which was not quite certain.

"That's right," said her dad. "Any moment."

"They're gone," said Patience. But she continued to stand in the garden at the foot of the dovecote, long after her mother and father had made cheery noises about tea, about waiting indoors, about giving the doves a chance to fly free.

After an hour, tears began to run down her cheeks, though she did not notice: her eyes were so sore from peering into the brightness of the sky. Her mother, who had been watching from the kitchen window, came out and led her indoors.

"They're gone, Mum. They're not coming back. I've lost them."

"If they have, it's no fault of yours," said Mum. "You were so patient. You waited longer than I would ever have done. Your father and I are so proud of the way you looked after them and didn't rush to set them free."

"They're gone, all the same," said Patience.

"We'll see," said her mother sadly. "Bedtime now."

Three

Next morning, Noah and Nelly were sitting in the doorway of the dovecote as if they owned not only the tall white spire but the garden and house and the whole village beyond it as well. They crooned and blinked and swivelled their heads round to the most preposterous angles, and only took off when Patience came to the kitchen door and squealed with delight at seeing them.

Mum had to put up a shelf on the house wall where the feeding troughs and water dish could be fastened. "Out of the way of cats," said Mum.

To and fro swooped Noah and Nelly, as if they were jumping a canyon: down to

the shelf, back up to the cote. The
sparrows and yellowhammers came
flocking, too, marvelling at the new array
of food suddenly put out for them. (They
only usually got the bacon rind and crusts
from breakfast.) But when the wood-
pigeons got wind of the news, and came
winging in low over the fence, Noah was
really put out.

It was the first time Patience noticed how much less nimble the doves were than the garden birds. Their magnificent fans of tail feathers and those great swelling chests did not allow for a quick take-off. Noah was like an emperor weighed down by ermine robes – splendid and regal, but slow. The darting little sparrows were bandits stealing from his treasury.

After a week or two, Nelly began to make fewer trips to the feeding shelf. She stayed in the dovecote more. Patience was worried about her – began to read the booklets entitled *Diseases of the Pigeon Family* and *Ailments Among Garden Fowl*.

It is never a good idea to read medical books. Soon she was lying awake at night thinking about worms and canker and coccidiosis. It was in bare feet and pyjamas that she went to the shed and got out the stepladder early one morning, before school, and peeped inside the dovecote with a torch.

Neither dove was home. Instead, there, on a mound of unsavoury bits and pieces, lay a small, perfect, slightly blue-shelled egg.

Patience was so surprised that she almost stepped back into thin air. The ladder wobbled alarmingly, and her hands and bare feet got all hot from the fright. Gingerly, she climbed down, her legs shaking with fright and delight. An egg! Noah and Nelly were going to hatch a squab!

"It may not be fertile," said her father.

"If all the eggs that hens lay were to hatch into chicks, we would be up to our armpits in chickens," said her mother. They wanted to save her disappointment.

34

But Patience was sure that Noah and Nelly's egg would hatch. She did not disturb the parents with any more nosy visits – not until enough days had gone by for the egg to have hatched. Even then, she discovered that if she lay down on the landing and looked through the low windows, she could just see a short way in at the door.

And there it was – an ugly pink morsel of birdy Play-Do: a squab. In her diary at school Patience wrote, *I now have THREE doves,* using capital letters and underlining it and leaning on her pencil so hard that she could read it on the page beneath and the one under that:

"THREE"

Tiger

Sometimes, instead of Neesha coming
round to play after school, Patience went
round to her house. It was only four
houses down the lane. Patience knew
Neesha's cat, Tiger, almost as well as she
knew Neesha. Sometimes she saw Tiger
balancing along her own garden fence: he
had glorious orange fur on the underside
of his plumy tail: a marmalade cat.

"Do you mean he eats marmalade?"
Patience had said the very first time the
friends met. They laughed about it, now
that they were grown up. Neesha could
still send them off into fits of giggles just
by saying it, and copying Patience's face.
"*Do you mean he eats marmalade?*"

It was a bitterly cold day at the end of autumn when Patience looked out of the window and saw Tiger walking along the fence. He jumped across into the horse chestnut tree, then down into the long grass behind the barbecue. What a jump! thought Patience.

Then she realised what Tiger was doing. From up above, she could see his marmalade back moving through the grass, keeping low, prowling round the side of the shed, that orange tail held at a strange angle. He was hunting the doves.

She hammered on the window. The cat looked up with an oddly guilty expression, then bolted away under the fence and into the lane. But when Patience looked out ten minutes later, he was there again, rounding the corner of the shed, watching Noah and Nelly and the squab feeding on the ground beneath the shelf.

Three at a time, Patience went down the stairs, through the living room into the kitchen. No key in the kitchen door! She had to go out through the washing-machine room, and she picked up the powder dispenser as she went, to throw at the cat.

The look in Tiger's green eyes was insolent now. He ran off when she threw the hollow plastic ball at him, but only as far as the fence. From there he walked off haughtily, tail waving, at a dignified pace, as if to say, *I can wait. I can come back whenever I choose. I am in no hurry.*

"You keep your cat out of my garden!" Patience said to Neesha the moment she saw her at school next day.

"He's a cat. He goes where he wants!" said Neesha with a laugh.

"He was trying to eat my doves!" snapped Patience, and Neesha saw that she was not joking.

"He's a cat," she said again and shrugged. But she did not like the way her friend looked at her. Patience had never glared at her like that before. Almost like a wild animal.

The thought of Tiger stalking her doves made Patience hot with anger every time it came to her. She and Neesha usually walked home together from school, but today Patience ran on ahead, without waiting for her friend to finish packing up her bag.

She filled all the cups in the kitchen with cold water, and found the key to the kitchen door, so that she could whip it open in a moment and toss a cup of water over the predatory cat. Perhaps if I scare him enough, he won't dare come round any more, she thought.

All of a sudden, her garden was a citadel – her territory – to be guarded against intruders, raiders, the attacking enemy: Tiger. She got out pan lids to clash together, unwound the garden hose. When her mother got home from work, an hour later, she looked around the kitchen – the armoury – in disbelief. "Patience, whatever is going on?"

"It's Neesha's horrible cat. It's after my doves! It's after Noah and Nelly and N—" She did not finish. She had named the squab after her best friend but it no longer seemed like a good idea. ". . . and Nanook," she ended.

"I thought the baby was going to be called Neesha," said her mother, putting away the pan lids.

"Nanook sounds more friendly," said Patience.

About a week later, just as Patience came in at the gate, a flash of orange came past in the opposite direction. She dropped her school bag and ran round the house. Noah and Nelly were sitting on the sill of the dovecote, breasts pressed together like Siamese twins, cheek to cheek, heads bobbing. The squab was nowhere to be seen.

Perhaps it was safe inside the dovecote. Perhaps the white feathers blowing about the lawn in the bitter wind were no more than Patience's family of doves moulted every day.

But there was no mistaking the red, messy bundle behind the hydrangea bushes. When she picked up Nanook's little dead body, the squab was still almost intact. After all, Tiger was a well-fed cat. He did not need to *eat* the birds he stalked.

The joy was simply in killing them.

Enemies

"I hate you," Patience screamed at Neesha, standing on her doorstep, hands made into fists by her side. "I hate your filthy cat and I hate you!"

Neesha blinked her large brown eyes and shut the door. There seemed no point in entering into a quarrel.

The trouble was, they had to see each other at school every day. They changed desks, so as not to have to sit together, but it was hard to avoid speaking, avoid working together on shared projects.

If Patience had known how, she would have killed Tiger. She craved revenge. But *people* are not allowed to go out on the prowl with murder in their hearts: only *cats* are allowed to do that. Nicely brought-up little girls are supposed to laugh and make up when they quarrel. Patience could see that her parents expected Neesha to come round any day and play again, for the feud to be forgotten. They did not realise how deep the hatred burned in Patience after finding that little dead bird.

Once again, Mrs Clarke was asking them to give a three-minute talk to the rest of the class. "Maybe you would like to tell us more about your doves, dear?" said Mrs Clarke, but Patience only shook her head. Fortunately, Mrs Clarke did not push anyone to speak if they did not want to. Normally, Neesha, for instance, was far too shy.

But today Neesha stood up, her fingers knotted together in front of her, her shoulders rounded in nervousness. "I would like to tell you about cats," she said.

Patience looked up, outraged, flaring
her nostrils, making her eyes blaze at
Neesha. Neesha ducked her face, but went
on in a strong, loud voice.

"All cats are related to tigers. They are hunters. Even domestic cats are just little tigers, you see. They have a territory – a whole street sometimes. Every day they patrol it. If another cat comes along, they fight to defend their patch of ground. Their heads are full of old memories, you see. They all remember being tigers. They all remember needing to hunt to feed themselves and their cubs. They can't forget. It is printed inside their eyelids – inside every cat's eyelids: '*I am a tiger.*' People call it instinct, but it's really the writing on their eyelids. '*I am a tiger. I hunt or I die.*'"

Neesha sat down, so suddenly that the classroom was quiet for ten whole seconds, not realising she had finished.

Mrs Clarke caught sight of the glance Neesha shot at Patience, and the stare which answered it.

"How lucky we are," the teacher said to her class, "not to have such killer instincts inside us. Or if we have," she added drily, "that we can get the better of them."

Noah and Nelly did not mourn half as long as Patience. Within days, Nelly was sitting on another egg. Another squab was on the way.

This was the most marvellous part of all for Patience. She could hardly comprehend the wonder of new life hatching out of that dirt-caked egg. She could not wait to see it. This time she would defend it from Tiger if she had to electrify the garden fence, dig traps in the lawn, put out poisoned cat meat . . . She could not wait to see the little, featherless, pink creature wriggling into life. She could not wait.

One icy day after school, though there was snow in the air and slippery patches of ice on the patio, Patience got out the stepladder again. Her mother was not home to forbid it; it was her day to work late. Up went Patience, and peeped into the dark cavity.

She startled Nelly, who was dozing on the nest, and who made a rush for the door. Patience snatched her head away just in time, and the ladder wobbled. Nelly fluttered down to the patio. Now Patience could see that the egg was not hatched. It was days overdue. It must be infertile: a blank.

Patience knew she ought to break the egg, so that Nelly would not waste her energy and devotion keeping brood over an infertile egg, but she did not want to. What if the birds hated her for doing it? Too awful to be hated by your friends . . .

Out of the corner of her eye, Patience saw a flicker of orange: Tiger was on the prowl! She took off her glove and threw it. The stepladder, perched as it was on a patch of ice, slid off the patio into the garden bed, and teetered over. Patience's head hit the underside of the dovecote, and she did not even put out a hand to save herself as the steps pitched over and fell flat across the dead underbrush of the winter garden.

When she woke up, she was in bed. She wondered if it had been one of those falling nightmares where you wake up before you hit the ground. Then she began to realise, from the various aches and pains up and down her body, that she must have hit some piece of ground very hard indeed, chiefly with her head.

Her mother was speaking to her, but for a while her face seemed to be speaking a foreign language without subtitles. Patience could make no sense of what was being said to her. Finally she fathomed it out: " . . . if it hadn't been for Neesha's cat . . . " Mum was saying.

Yes, thought Patience bitterly. If it hadn't been for that brute Tiger.

" . . . The doctor said the cold was the biggest danger. Lying out there unconscious, in the cold for two hours and more. If Tiger hadn't curled up on your chest and kept you warm . . . "

Neesha came to visit her at home every day; Patience was off school for a whole week. Sometimes Tiger chose to visit as well (though he was an independent beast, and could not be relied on). Sometimes, they all three sat on the landing and watched the doves – whiter than the snow on the garden lawn – though the frustration of it drove the cat into a frenzy of roaring, and he pawed at the glass, trying to reach the distant doves, the falling snowflakes.

"I'll try to keep him away," said Neesha. "I honestly will."

"Oh, so will I," said Patience, resting a hand on the scruff of the cat's neck and fondling his ears. "Believe me, so will I."